Silk Egg

Silk Egg

Collected Novels
(2009–2009)

Eileen R. Tabios

Shearsman Books
Exeter

First published in the United Kingdom in 2011 by
Shearsman Books
58 Velwell Road
Exeter EX4 4LD

www.shearsman.com

ISBN 978-1-84861-143-6

Front Cover image: 'Untitled' (2003) by Maureen McQuillan.
(10"x 8" ink and acrylic on paper).

Acknowledgements
See page 130.

for Mei-mei Berssenbrugge, Arthur Sze and John Yau
whose innovative outlooks helped me years ago to find a path
that led to this book

and

for Philip Lamantia who, in response to my complaint over not
being able to draw a straight line, replied, "Draw a curve."

Contents

Silk Egg / 9
Pewter / 19
Cambodia / 29
Rarefied / 39
Stubborn Entry / 49
Dear Cloud / 59
Modern Tulips / 69
Opium-Scented Lace / 79
Same Ol' Argument / 89
Christmas / 99
Lack / 109
Novel Chatelaine / 119

Selected Notes / 128
Acknowledgements / 130
About the Author / 131

Silk Egg

Chapter I

At the most infinitesimal hint of light, she closed like a purple mirabilis jalapa folding petals into a frozen fist.

Her birthland is replete with child soldiers.

Chapter II

A thick glass tumbler bearing ice and amber looked cheerfully judicial.

Pronounced "rehabilitated," he was allowed to accompany her home.

Her bedroom was designed as an egg. Hence, silk walls of a pale blue once discerned staining Antarctic ice.

He moved into her gift, woke each morning to soft warm lucidity, and agreed as regards the irrelevance of ribbons.

Chapter III

Once, there was biology.

It produced a mother whose absence was a singe.

It sang.

It replaced marrow—a song camouflaged by inevitably aging bone.

Chapter IV

With his watch on her mahogany night stand, she no longer longed for blue streaks to blossom from her hair. *Realism*, she conceded, can suddenly become synonym for *Desire*.

Chapter V

Look where the window view finally stops.
"Sky is better than aspirin."

Chapter VI

The evenings are always pleasingly raw.
Air forgets to chill.

Chapter VII

They both forget to dream about empty chairs.

They both forget to dream of a long-haired lady in a white taffeta gown, ignored in a hotel lobby as she strums and croons to a gilded harpsichord.

Pewter

Chapter I

A pewter sea.

No consolation.

That day, Saudi Arabia cooperated with Israel against Washington.

Chapter II

The dart sliced the orchid before the target fell.

Blood against Savile Row.

Déjà vu.

Chapter III

So much to be learned about human history by merely knowing Aristarchus thought that the sun, not the earth, was the center of the universe. And that Copernicus, who gazed 17 centuries later, is credited with that revelation.

Chapter IV

Asters, wax bells, goldenrod, pansies and mums bloomed from decorative pots.

Much consolation.

Birdsong—*no edge to the sound of it* . . .

Much, much consolation.

Chapter V

She thinks of her daughter who would have been 19 today. Ever on the brink of womanhood, with the sunlight ever on her hair. And ever glinting back from sapphire eyes.

She remembers and Mercury slowly hijacks her veins.

Chapter VI

She lifts the hand with its faux wedding band. Next to a faux engagement ring of blue sapphire surrounded by diamonds. She lifts her hand to wave.

He sees her. He smiles.

Chapter VII

He saw her, smiled, and approached.

For the last time, her ringless hand reached for the grim metal in the pocket of her magenta silk skirt.

Heat.

He was also confused by the last thing he heard: *Fool: one should never want obedience to be blind.*

Cambodia

Chapter I

He was sipping honeysuckle in a fluted crystal, its glass as thin as pre-birth membrane.

A shirt woven from hummingbird wings, she thought as she approached, right hand clutching a blue, fraying velvet purse.

Chapter II

"Au contraire. *You* glow," he would come to whisper.

A witness shivered.

As for the rest of it, San Francisco sparkled. Cheerful strangers caped them with cheerful words flitting through the Vietnamese restaurant.

Chapter III

It should have been Bolinas, or as Jim Carroll once put it, "Bo Diddleyville."

The restaurant served a metaphor for a country.

Once, that country received refugees.

Chapter IV

She remembered.

Ultimately, she could not fight memory.

Someone once shared, "I can count every rib in my rib cage, but my stomach protrudes outward, bloated like a ball between my chest and hips. The flesh on my feet is so swollen it glistens as if it will pop open. Curious, I push my thumb into my swollen feet, pressing the flesh inward and creating a big dent. Counting under my breath I wait to see how long it takes for the dent to fill itself up. After a while, I make more dents on my feet, legs, arms, and face. My body is like a balloon. The dents I make reinflate slowly."

Chapter V

He defined "genius" as "beef with mint sauce."
She felt no resentment.

Chapter VI

However, she prodded, "The landmines still exist."

The lace bordering the purse's handles had come unstitched in places so that it hung in tatters.

Chapter VII

He realized how much he agreed when he heard himself whisper, "Accurate maps must be amoral."

Rarefied

Chapter I

Red velvet petals. On one, a wet diamond.

Her shears also sliced the sun.

Six roses fell. All revealed red cracking into mother-of-pearl.

London seemed even more distant that day.

Chapter II

"The more you cut off from extremities, the more potential for growth," once, he tossed at her while turning a page of *The Wall Street Journal*.

She replied, "We are discussing rose bushes, are we not?"

She replied without irony.

The room was decorated with assortments of greenery and topped by a ceiling of iron and thick glass. Here and there, depending on the shifting light, glass panes revealed thin, gold veins.

Chapter III

A newspaper shrugged as the Dow fell for the eighth day in a row.

St. Johns—its dappled turquoise contexts—suddenly felt like a dream instead of an island.

Chapter IV

In the too-near future, she will whisper over a river
flowing beneath an arched bridge cast from ancient stones,
"Paris never revealed its warmth."

She will loosen a bracelet and watch jade penetrate water,
its wake to be defined by moss.

Chapter V

Here, one narrator could lapse to French but that would be pretentious. *Kann man zu bewusst sein?* Someone thinks to question air. For air bears no grudges.

Chapter VI

She smiles at the waiter depositing a stack of wholewheat blinis on the corseted table.

As ever, the different perfumes in the room failed to clash—this is a place for conspiracy as marked by the feathers and snake skins of socialites.

Which is the stronger armor? Loneliness or pride?

Chapter VII

He decided to bother to articulate what he thought should be obvious by now: "If the city is tedious, let's spend the weekend in the country."

After a moment long enough for her gaze to take in the panorama of the high-ceilinged room he favored, she nodded agreeably. But replied, "*If* that's where radiance absconded."

Stubborn Entry

Chapter I

Her lid fell like a wave. A tear obviated the wink.
Thus, did she become my horizon.

Chapter II

A beautiful murderer coiled against the front door.

Beneath moonlight, the green of its skin deliquesced to a silver necklace lost in childhood.

The next time he saw her, she wore the rattlesnake skin as a bracelet for her enchantingly slim ankle.

Chapter III

Her collarbone jutted like the tip of a snow-packed mountain he never straddled with his eyes fixated on the rubies he promised her but diverted to an orchid-perfumed terrorist with philosophical eyes.

Chapter IV

Is it as gold as Rome or as gold as Paris?

Chapter V

She made my finger leave its memories of the interior of my German Shepherd's ears—that velvety flesh with silken threads.

Against Gabriela's puppy ears, even new shoes lose their power.

Chapter VI

The balls of Lindt white chocolate truffles melted within her suddenly avaricious mouth.

She wore lipstick that day named "Raspberry Moonshine."

His cock was midnight.

Chapter VII

The conclusion is a red skull and, *Oh! How it lit up that corner of the room!*

Where a staircase led up to a higher part of the wall and it is a greedy disillusion that would sculpt that impassive space into a *Door*.

Dear Cloud

Chapter I

Clouds. A poet's mother called them "puffballs." Soft
cotton balls. How can something so soft be dangerous when
contextualized under X-ray to be interruption of bone?

Chapter II

Her mirrors hear many thoughts unspoken to others. Like, "What does it mean that Daddy had to die before I could become big enough to be a parent?"

Chapter III

Her father died of brain cancer. She wrote a 366-page poetry book about what she continually failed to say, even as she knew he *longed* to hear.

The title begins, *The Light Sang* . . .

Chapter IV

Clouds.

As necessary to sunlit, blue sky as horizon.

She practices religion by believing, *There's nothing so sad as a false metaphor.*

As pointless as skim milk flowing briefly into Senegalese coffee.

Chapter V

Carl Andre once said, *I do not, in my poetry, try to find the words to express what I want to say. In my poetry, I try to find ways to express what the words say.*

Still. Some words can never be just words. For example? An adjective based on ethnicity. Like "Guam," used just twice in an English poem and in both instances meant to be a synonym for a "stopping point" on the way elsewhere. A pass-over.

A pause.

As if no island existed with its specific body, history and people.

As if words can erase . . .

Chapter VI

A "puffball" killed my father. A white cloud as soft as his daughter who nonetheless also killed him.

Where is the comfort to your whispered, "Life causes death"?

Chapter VII

You are approaching me with an oversized white ceramic cup on saucer. Steam rises from your hand.

You place before me your offering: "a low fat café au lait, just as I know you like it."

I look down to a white puffball frothed from skim milk.

I force myself to smile at the cloud. Still. Soon, my hair to be a soft cloud loosening rain, rain, rain.

Modern Tulips

Chapter I

The tulips reminded her of the philosopher reminded by tulips of vagina dentata.

Chapter II

The philosopher continued to water the magenta bulbs as he ranted at the phone camera.

One of the rare times, she muses, *that attention deficit disorder didn't pop up as a likely cause.*

Chapter III

Can the flower feel the edge of scissors against its stalk?

Chapter IV

Backdrop hijacks foreground, transforms transparencies to colors. Colors become compromised into bodies.

Chapter V

Except.

Not all days need be empty, she thinks, painting her lips with crushed pearls and magenta wax.

Chapter VI

She becomes a pale neck encircled by cartoon-perfect diamonds. Drapes open in the hotel room to reveal the twinkling Manhattan skyline.

She asks her reflection, *What is a "suburb"?*

Chapter VII

Fresh from the mahogany-inlaid bar, he raises his gaze from the black silk on the floor. Looking at her swollen lips, he observes:

"This is the knowledge we share: *the heart is pure animal.*"

Opium-Scented Lace

Chapter I

Whenever surf broke and water pock-marked air, she recalled Helen—the much-maligned Helen.

Surf broke to reveal pale ankles bound by thin strips of gold-painted leather.

Chapter II

She promised the mirror, *As an old woman, I shall lack doilies in my legacy.*

Chapter III

The mirror leered.

She remembered Greece: Aegean sea, clean lapis lazuli sky, white cotton curtains billowing over ecstatic shadows. And a ruby necklace.

She swatted at the mirror, a computer screen.

The clasp to the ruby necklace had broken. When the necklace fell to the stone floor, not a single ruby shattered.

Chapter IV

A quest. Sheep. Warriors wearing farmers' boots.

A quest.

Mud. Then fleece.

Chapter V

Dismayed, she realized she spent much of her working hours at the internet café surfing for something in order to make something exist. Her name was Madonna.

The café was owned by a granddaughter of Romanian gypsies. She banned cigarillos. She worked out five times a week at the local gym. She was kind. The café owner's name was relegated to initials: H.D.

Living a good life, someone once whispered in a childhood schoolyard, *is one conclusion to a grave secret.*

Chapter VI

The next day, Madonna brought a box of books to H.D. She deposited them by the cash register that H.D. was trying to fix for the umpteenth time.

"What's this?" H.D. looked up, the lack of lipstick only enhancing the fullness of her lips.

"Some of my books," Madonna replied, then went over to the computer in the corner where she spent much of her hours.

Chapter VII

H.D. cleared a shelf in the café for Madonna's books

Dramatically sweeping a shelf clean of its plastic bowls, she declared: "Down with Tupperware!"

Once, H.D. had suggested to Madonna that it would be cheaper for her if she owned her own computer.

Madonna had replied with the obvious, "Mobility requires money . . ."

Same Ol' Argument

Chapter I

Ironically, a lighthouse provided the setting.

When the ocean is angry, the island would be halved by high tides—as was the case that evening while another storm also raged.

The tapestry with its earth-toned palette and maiden in white failed to keep the chill away from the stone walls.

Chapter II

She wished the lightning flash didn't reveal his eyes.

Chapter III

His eyes were those of a different man when they first saw her. She had been sitting on the museum's marble steps—silk, velvet, pearls and musk perfume flowing about her as she leaned to peruse a broken heel.

Around them swirled billionaire hedge fund managers in black tuxedos escorted by tall tulips alternating diamonds with sapphires. The women had learned the importance of contrast when they studied style, otherwise they might not have bothered to adjust the all-diamond strands cuffed about their necks and wrists, or emeralds piercing their flesh in visible and/or silk-hidden places.

His eyes dismissed them all to narrow the world into an image of full scarlet lips juxtaposed against a pale ankle. His eyes also dismissed the shoe, broken but still lovely in coral suede.

Chapter IV

Now, the world narrowed to the image of a small hand clutching the back of a chair.

For support, he realized, startled.

Chapter V

He smoothed the grimness he felt on his face. He hooded his eyes.

She felt the easing from the landscape she'd memorized with her lips.

Chapter VI

She'd memorized his face as—head flung back—he'd laughed, and laughed, and laughed.

Chapter VII

That he would later grouse, "All love stories are the same cliché" did not dampen the immense satisfaction that had returned to the interior of the lighthouse.

Outside, the world shivered from a wet black fog—a suffering become tolerant, if not actually irrelevant.

Christmas

Chapter I

Faded, but the price sticker still clung to the antique brooch.

Its presence replicated something floating as a splinter within the murk of a river, or her mind.

Somewhere, burgundy brooded.

Chapter II

She knows what can drain gold from metal: *Touch*.

At the local library, an artist is exhibiting ancient handkerchiefs embossed with black-and-white photographs. Shelves of skulls fade behind matters of aesthetics.

Pristine linen and found photographs share something in common: only fools trust them.

I speak as someone too familiar with the "edges of my body."

Chapter III

The popular media is wrong. Courtly men are usually trustworthy. Like unfrayed cuffs ending and edging dark wool pants.

Which doesn't make me less tired of reading women's gospels outside of the *Holy Bible*.

Chapter IV

When she called me "lovely" it was to create for me a different life. But resentment usually arises at *recognized* motivations.

Chapter V

Cool water calms so ethereally.
Miracles are fragile.

Chapter VI

At age twenty-four she stopped layering lotion against her flesh.

"God," she said, "is who I shout for."

"P.S." she added. "Screw the timorousness of the infidel's 'small g'."

Chapter VII

Is it any wonder that Christmas, though but a spangled veil, is welcome.

Lack

Chapter I

"As regards the matter of clocks . . ." she tries again, but pauses at his grin.

Jerk, she thinks as she recovers her stare and turns it inward to the past, the only thing they now share.

He sees her touch her throat with a delicate finger.

Chapter II

Once, she carved out a week her Blackberry was reluctant to yield. She gave him the week with a silver box encircled by ribbons cut from a red and green plaid fabric.

Chapter III

"Souvenir" becomes defined as an assortment of ribbons.

Chapter IV

The burgundian silk once flowed into a huge, floppy bow that he untied. Then wrapped around her eyes.

Afterwards, he conceded, "Yes, color has a scent . . ."

Chapter V

"...which I would like not to become a matter of elephants gingerly tip-toed on circus blocks," she continues today as if the lack between them had not interrupted.

Chapter VI

"Sentimentality is a weakness," he replies, the interior of his mouth souring at the cliché.

"Not to worry," she says. "I am not an addict."

Chapter VII

Pause.

A mutual mental shift snags something, as when a man tosses aside a black tie decorated with a pattern of violet stirrups to favor a tie with alternating lime and lemon polka dots.

The opposite of lack can be worse.

She crosses her legs bolstered by opaque silk while he uncrosses his muscles armored in pin-striped wool. Lawyers begin to speak for the first time.

Novel Chatelaine

Chapter I

It began with the recollection of a blue silk pocket.

From which an iron key fell.

Which made her purr, "Well hello you 17th Century ...!"

Chapter II

Each window of the limestone chateaux offered the view of a vineyard where leaves had turned a radioactive shade of orange because of the old geezer's neglect.

Chapter III

"Compassion" is defined as forgiving an old man for fearing his mortality whenever an inspector noted, "You should replace those vines."

Chapter IV

On a table in a dim room in the bowels of a wine cellar created by gigantic steel blades penetrating a stone mountain, hordes of decanters waited beneath dust cloaks.

Chapter V

So it came that, one evening, he returned to a clean dining room resplendent with new velvet drapes, several large crystal vases overflowing with red roses, and a sparkling chandelier fashioned from gold antlers.

Chapter VI

"Nihilism is lazy," she announced cheerfully between mouthfuls of what once was boar.

(Nearby, needless to say, breathed the 1950 Pétrus.)

Chapter VII

The following morning, he forgot the crumbling temples of his knees to pick up a shovel.

He dug into the ground to cut the first of what would be many toppled old vines by the time the day deliquesced to cricket song.

He cut the earth with absolutely no remorse. Remorse absolutely zero.

Selected Notes

Cambodia

In Chapter III, the Jim Carroll quote is from *Forced Entries: The Downtown Diaries 1971–1973* by Jim Carroll (Penguin, New York, 1987).

In Chapter IV, the quote is from *First They Killed My Father: A Daughter of Cambodia Remembers* by Loung Ung (HarperCollins, New York, 2000).

Dear Cloud

In Chapter I, the concept of clouds as puffballs is from *The Middle Room* by Jennifer Moxley (Subpress, Oakland, CA, 2007).

In Chapter III, "*The Light Sang . . .*" references the author's *THE LIGHT SANG AS IT LEFT YOUR EYES: Our Autobiography* (Marsh Hawk Press, New York, 2007).

In Chapter V, the reference to Guam is from the following excerpt in Craig Santos Perez's review of Oliver de la Paz's *Names Above Houses* published in *Galatea Resurrects (A Poetry Engagement)*, Aug. 30, 2007: "Since I am from Guam, and also moved from Guam to the American States at a young age, it was striking to me that de la Paz includes my homeland in this poem. In my own limited readings, this is only the second time I have encountered "Guam" in a poem by someone not from Guam (the other is Robert Duncan's 'Uprising: Passages 25'). In both cases, Guam is represented as simply a place to pass, either a migratory passage from Asia to America, or in Duncan's case, a military passage from the U.S. military bases on Guam to Asia (during the Vietnam War). This is not meant to indict either Duncan or de la Paz for their superficial representations of Guam, but merely to displace, for a moment, the hegemonic representation of Guam as simply a site of passage for others."

Modern Tulips

In Chapter I, the referenced philosopher is Slavoj Žižek.

Pewter

Written after *The Alexandria Link* by Steve Berry (Ballantine Books, New York, 2007).

Rarefied

In Chapter V, "Kann man zu bewusst sein?" translates to "Can one be too aware?"

Silk Egg

The second sentence in Chapter I is written after *A Long Way Gone: Memoirs of a Boy Soldier* by Ishmael Beah (Sarah Crichton Books/Farrar, Straus & Giroux).

Acknowledgements

Thanks to the following publications and their editors which first published the following novels:

Dear Cloud
—*OurOwnVoice* (2010), Eds. Reme Grefalda and Aileen Ibardaloza, as part of presentation as *OurOwnVoice*'s Resident Poet 2010

Modern Tulips
—*Moria: a poetry journal* (Chicago, 2010), Ed. William Allegrezza

Pewter
—*MiPOesias*, Summer 2010, Ed. Didi Menendez

Silk Egg
—*Cerise Press: A Journal of Literature, Arts & Culture*, Fall 2009, Issue 2 (Omaha & Paris), Eds. Greta Aart, Sally Molini and Karen Rigby. (Thanks, too, for the nomination for *Best American Short Stories* and *Best of the Net*.)

The inaugural novel of this project, *Novel Chatelaine*, was first published as a chapbook by TeenyTiny Press (Washington, 2009), Ed. Amanda Laughland.

Christmas was first published as a booklet by tiny booklets by chapbookpublisher.com (Kingston, PA, 2010), Ed. Dan Waber.

Agyamanac Unay to Barry Schwabsky for looking over this manuscript, then offering his own words in response. Deep gratitude as well to Tony Frazer of Shearsman Books for welcoming this book.

Last but never least, I am grateful for the company of poets whose support—and own writings—have been invaluable over the years, including but not limited to those mentioned above as well as Thomas A. Fink, Sandy McIntosh, Michelle Bautista, Eric Gamalinda, Bino A. Realuyo, Jukka-Pekka Kervinen, Leny M. Strobel, Jean Vengua, and Mark Young.

About the Author

Eileen R. Tabios has released 18 print, 4 electronic and 1 CD poetry collections, an art-essay collection, a poetry essay/interview anthology, a short story book and a collection of novels. Recipient of the Philippines' National Book Award for Poetry for her first poetry book *Beyond Life Sentences*, she has exhibited visual poetry and visual art throughout the United States and Asia. She's also edited, co-edited or conceptualized nine anthologies of poetry, fiction and essays.

Honors for her authored and edited works include the PEN/Oakland-Josephine Miles National Literary Award, The Potrero Nuevo Fund Prize, the Gustavus Meyers Outstanding Book Award in the Advancement of Human Rights, *Foreword Magazine* Anthology of the Year Award, *Poet Magazine's* Iva Mary Williams Poetry Award, Judds Hill's Annual Poetry Prize and the Philippine American Writers & Artists' Catalagan Award; recognition from the Academy of American Poets, the Asian Pacific Association of Librarians and the PEN-Open Book Committee; as well as grants from the Witter Bynner Foundation, National Endowment of the Arts, the New York State Council on the Humanities, the California Council for the Humanities, and the New York City Downtown Cultural Council.

Ms. Tabios has crafted a body of work that is unique for melding ekphrasis with transcolonialism. Her poems have been translated into Spanish, Italian, Tagalog, Japanese, Portuguese, Polish, Greek, computer-generated hybrid languages, Paintings, Video, Drawings, Visual Poetry, Mixed Media Collages, Kali Martial Arts, Music, Modern Dance and Sculpture. As part of her poetry-as-performance approach, she blogs as the "Chatelaine" at http://angelicpoker.blogspot.com and edits *Galatea Resurrects (A Poetry Engagement)*, a popular poetry review journal at http://galatearesurrects.blogspot.com

As a further extension of her poetics, she also founded Meritage Press (http://www.meritagepress.com), a multi-disciplinary literary and arts press based in San Francisco & St. Helena.

www.ingramcontent.com/pod-product-compliance
Lightning Source LLC
Chambersburg PA
CBHW030337020726
47493CB00004B/1307

* 9 7 8 1 8 4 8 6 1 1 4 3 6 *